W9-BUC-595

LEGENDS
OF ZITA
THE SPACEGIRL

New York & London

Published by First Second
First Second is an imprint of Roaring Brook Press,
a division of Holtzbrinck Publishing Holdings Limited Partnership
175 Fifth Avenue, New York, New York 10010

Distributed in the United Kingdom by Macmillan Children's Books,
a division of Pan Macmillan.

Cover and interior design by Colleen AF Venable

Cataloging-in-Publication Data is on file at the Library of Congress

Paperback ISBN: 978-1-59643-447-9
Hardcover ISBN: 978-1-59643-806-4

First Second books are available for special promotions and premiums.
For details, contact: Director of Special Markets, Holtzbrinck Publishers.

First Edition 2012

Printed in China by Macmillan Production (Asia) Ltd., Kwun Tong, Kowloon, Hong Kong
(supplier code 10)

Paperback: 10 9 8 7 6 5 4 3 2 1
Hardcover: 10 9 8 7 6 5 4 3 2 1

:01
First Second
New York & London

Much after a beginning is difficult, as everybody knows who has crossed the sea, and as for the first step a man never so much as remembers it...

...The first step is undertaken lightly, pleasantly, and with your soul in the sky; it is the five-hundredth that counts.

—Hillaire Belloc

SCRIK
SCRIK
imprint-
o-tron
holo-cable
included
RECALLED

SHOOF!

PUT
PUT
PUT

PUT
PUT

PUT
PUT
PUT
PUT
PUT

ZITA!
THE GIRL WHO SAVED SCRIPTORIUS!
ONE DAY ONLY!
PUT
PUT
PUT
PUT
CLICK.

CRACK!

SCHLOMP
SCHLOMP

LADYM's
TRAVELIN
SHOW
CLOP
CLOP
CLOP

ZITA THE SPACEGIRL!

HER SHIP JUST TOUCHED DOWN.

S'RIGHT! GONNA BEAT THE CROWDS!

'SKEWSUS!
JONK.

SHOVE!

JONK!

KA-
CHAK!

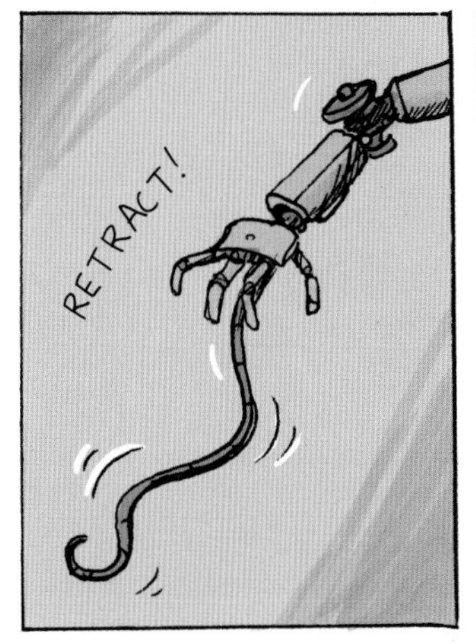
RETRACT!

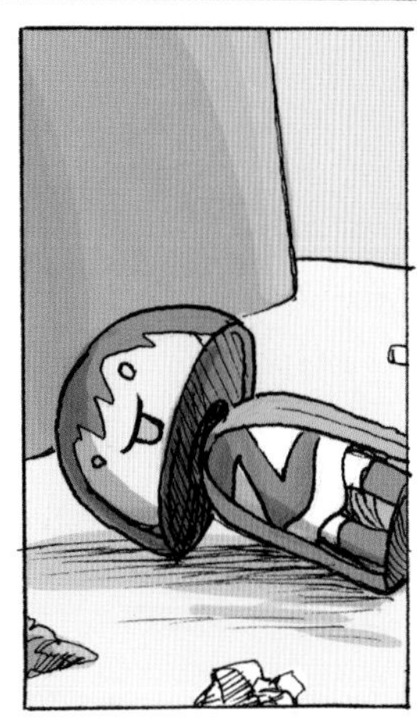

LADY M's
TRAVELING
SHOW

NAH!
WE DIN' BEAT THE CROWDS.

SNICKER!
WIN

LADIES AND GENTLEMEN! ANDROIDS OF EVERY KIND!

STEP RIGHT UP! DON'T BE SHY!

NOW MEET THE LEGEND!
UH.
HEH HEH...
WHAT IS THIS?
SOME KINDA TRICK?
GRRR ..
WE WANT ZITA!!

ZITA!

THERE'S A CROWD WAITING!

WAITING FOR YOU!

CREAK

THERE SHE IS!

IT'S HER! IT'S ZITA!
ZITA!
ZITA THE SPACEGIRL!

TELL US HOW YOU CAME FROM ACROSS THE UNIVERSE TO SAVE SCRIPTORIUS FROM THE ASTEROID!

I HEARD SHE PUNCHED IT WITH HER FISTS.
NAW! THAT AIN'T TRUE! SHE USED HER RAINBOW POWERS!

I WAS JUST TRYING TO SAVE MY FRIEND!
I DIDN'T DESTROY THE ASTEROID AT ALL,

IT WAS ROBOT RANDY.
HE'S A POWERFUL WEAPON.

RATTLE

HA HA HA!
WOO HOO HOO!
HA HA!

WHAT a SENSa HEWMa!

ZITa!
OVER HERE!

YOU COULD TaKE ME ON YOUR aDVENTURES!
I CaN STOMP J-JUS' LIKE YOU!
HUH! HUP!
Tap tap.

aDVENTURES...
BaH!

AND THANK YOU FOR YOUR KIND DONATION.

MORE AUTOGRAPHS?
GLOOP!
GLOOP!

AACK!
GLOOP!

GLOOP! GLOOP! GLOOP!

I'M JUST SAYING THAT MY SIGN HAS A CERTAIN GRAVITAS.
SECURITY
SECRTY
GLOOP
GLOOP!

HNH.

WHEW!

PUT-PUT CLICK

EEP!

DID - DID YOU MAKE THAT COSTUME YOURSELF?

IT'S PRETTY GOOD.

HEY, WHAT'S THAT?
W-WHAT ARE YOU DOING?

SZZT!

STOP IT!

VVVVT!

WHOa.

YOU LOOK JUST LIKE ME.

ZITa!

UH-OH.
WHERE'D SHE GO?
ZITa!

I GOTTA GO.

UNLESS...

YOU COULD GO OUT THERE FOR ME!
JUST FOR A BIT!

IT'S EASY! ALL YOU HAVE TO DO IS SMILE AND WAVE.

IT'S HER!
SHE'S BACK!
HOORAY!

PLINK!

HEY MOUSE!
LET'S GO HAVE SOME FUN!

Ha Ha!

LET'S NOT WASTE IT.

♫

I BET YOU'VE SAVED MORE'N A HUNNERT PLANETS!
HAVE YOU ALWAYS BEEN A HERO?

. . .
ALWAYS BEEN A HERO.

HA HA! I THOUGHT AS MUCH.
GOOD WORK, KID.

ALL RIGHT, ZITA. IT'S TIME FOR US TO-
MAKE WAY!

MAKE WAY FOR THE LUMPONIAN AMBASSADORS!

IT'S YOU!
WE'VE TRAVELED SO FAR TO FIND YOU!

OUR PLANET IS IN TERRIBLE DANGER!
TERRIBLE!

ONLY ZITA THE SPACEGIRL CAN SAVE US!
ONLY ZITA THE SPACEGIRL.

NOW HOLD ON.

JUST WHAT IS THIS TERRIBLE DANGER?
AND WHAT'S IN IT FOR US IF WE HELP YOU?

STAR HEARTS.

A SWARM OF THEM!
HEADED FOR NEW LUMPONIA!

STAR HEARTS-!

I-
I THINK YOU'VE MISJUDGED US.

I MEAN, ASTEROIDS ARE ONE THING, BUT STAR HEARTS...
THOUGHT SHE WAS A HERO.

STAR HEARTS WILL STRIP A PLANET DOWN TO BEDROCK IN UNDER A SOLAR CYCLE.
THEY ARE UNSTOPPABLE.

THEN OUR WORLD IS DOOMED.
ZITA THE SPACEGIRL WAS OUR LAST HOPE.

I WILL DO IT.

ZITA WILL SAVE YOUR WORLD.

HOORAY!
HOORAY FOR ZITA!

WE KNEW YOU WOULD SAVE US!

AND WAIT UNTIL YOU SEE THE TREASURE WE OFFER IN RETURN!

LADY MADRIGALS

TICKETS

TICKE

GOX.

ADMISSION

?

ca-CLICK!

WAH!
5
8

SHWING!
I'LL SAVE YOU, JO-JO!
OH NO!
5
8

PUNCH!

UGH!

AAH!

I-IM NOT WHO YOU THINK! I MEAN-
Snif

-OH.

TICKETS TO THE CIRCUS?
ADMIT ONE
THANK-

-YOU?

HURRR.

THERE'S OUR SEAT.

WAK
WAK
WAK
WAK
WAK
WAK

POP!
POP!
POP
POP!
DOP!
WAK!
WAK!
Ha!

DOP!
BONG!

SWIPE!

FSSSSS!

BOOM!

DA-DAA!

HOLD ON! I WANT TO SEE THE NEXT ACT.

POOF!

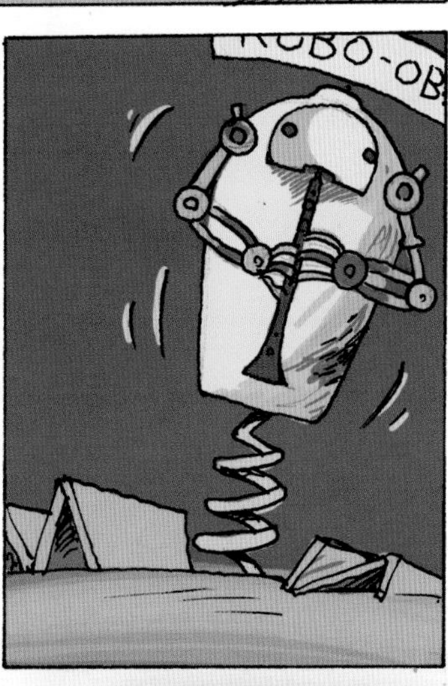

ROBO-OBO

FOOSH!

MOUSE, STOP!

CHING!

WAK! WAK!
HURRY!
WAK!

GLOVES
TRY 'EM
MULTIPLE FINGERS!
THUMBS TOO!
UP TO FORTY-SEVEN DIGITS.
HAS THE SPARKLE!!

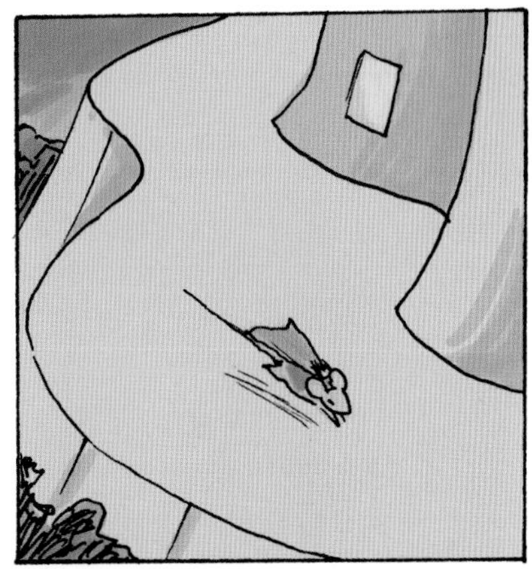

KNOCK
KNOCK

GREAT. IT'S YOU.

WE HAD BETTER SWITCH BACK BEFORE THE SHIP TAKES OFF.

C'MON, IT SOUNDS LIKE PIPER'S STARTED THE LAUNCH SEQUENCE.
SQUEEZE

WH-? HEY! WHAT ARE YOU DOING?!?

NGH!
!

SHOVE
AAK!

CLOSE

Chapter
Two

PFF!
LOOK AT THIS.
SLEEPIN' IN THE STREET.

THAT'S THE WAY THIS PLANET IS HEADED.

I BEEN SAYIN' IT FOR YEARS.

OHMYGOSH!
YOU OKAY, KID?
KID?

THEY LEFT WITHOUT ME!

YOU MISSED SEEIN' ZITA. IZZAT IT?
I AM ZITA!

NICE TRY, KID.

THE REAL ZITA IS OFF SAVIN' ANOTHER PLANET.

THEY SAY IT'S HER LAST ADVENTURE.

WHAT?
WHAT DO YOU MEAN?

TURNS OUT THE LUMPONIANS HAVE ONE OF THE LAST JUMP CRYSTALS.

AFTER ZITA SAVES THEIR WORLD-

-THEY'RE GONNA SEND HER HOME.

MOUSE!

MOUSE, THEY LEFT WITHOUT US!
AND IF WE DON'T CATCH THEM-

THEY'LL SEND THE ROBOT TO EARTH INSTEAD OF ME!

AND WITHOUT A SPACESHIP WE'RE TRAPPED HERE!
WE'LL BE STUCK ON THIS PLANET TILL WE'RE OLD!

CHING!

YOU'RE A GENIUS, PIZZICATO.

OH NO YOU DON'T!
OH YES I DO!

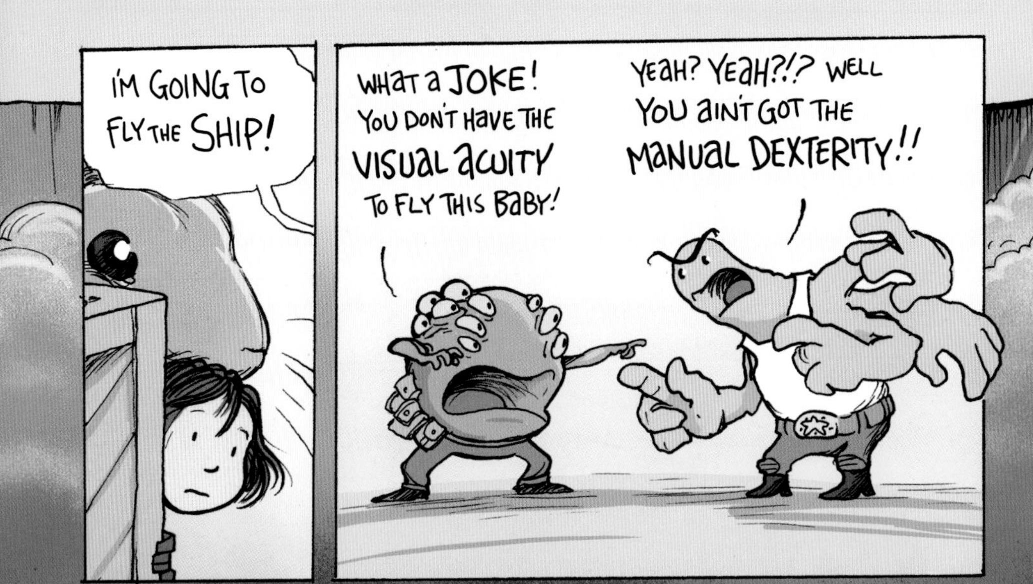

WHAT THIS SHIP NEEDS IS SHARP EYES LOOKIN' OUT FOR HER!

HA! WHAT SHE NEEDS IS STRONG GUIDING HANDS!
ARE YOU COMING?
CHEEP!

I'M NOT ASKING THEIR PERMISSION, IF THAT'S WHAT YOU MEAN.
IN OR OUT, MOUSE.
CLIK
CLIK

GET YER PAWS OFFA ME!
CH
CH

VOOM!

OUR SHIP!
THIEF!

CHIRRIP!
I'M TRYING! I'M TRYING!

CHANG
OOPS!

STEER!

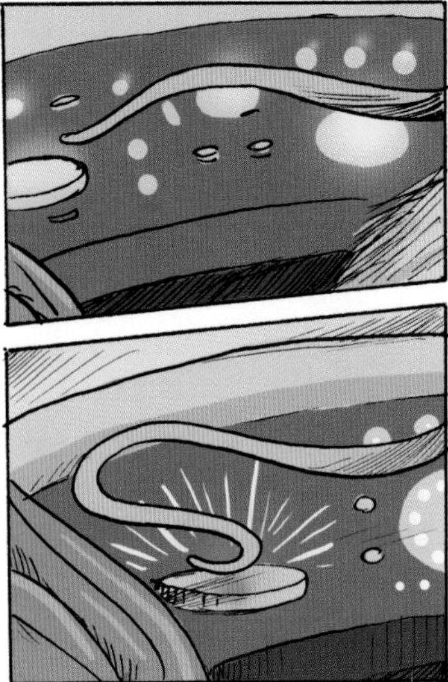

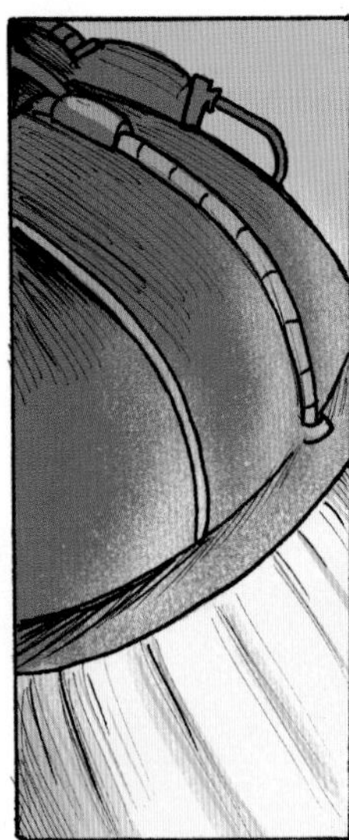

DID YOU SEE WHAT SHE DID TO OUR PAINT JOB?!?
WAIT'LL I GET MY HANDS ON HER!

HELLO DOOM SQUAD?

I'D LIKE TO REPORT A CRIME.

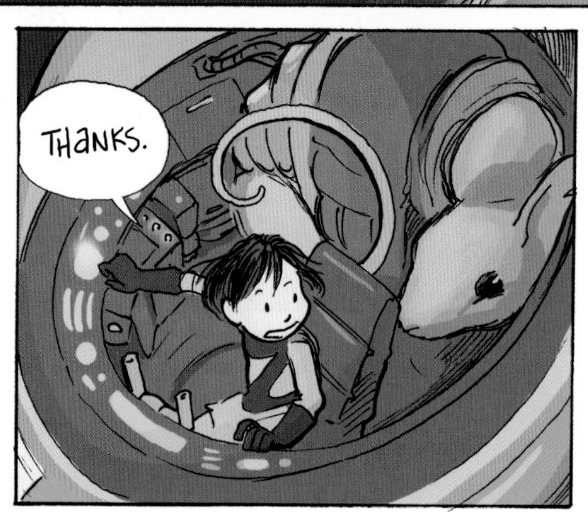
THANKS.

CHING!

we're criminals

BUT WE HAD NO CHOICE!

ATTENTION!
STOLEN VESSEL-

CUT YOUR ENGINES AND PREPARE TO BE BOARDED.

THAT'S THE WAY, CHIEF! TELL 'EM WITH AUTHORITY!
WILL YOU SIT BACK DOWN, STANLEY?

AN' FASTEN YOUR SECURITY BELT OR I'LL-
eh?

GREAT.

I THINK WE LOST THEM.

PIPER WAS PLANNING TO STOP AT THE NEXT TRADING POST.
MAYBE WE CAN GET THERE BEFORE THOSE GUYS CATCH US.

IT'S A FEW HOURS FROM HERE.
WE SHOULD GET SOME-
Z!

ZZZZZZ

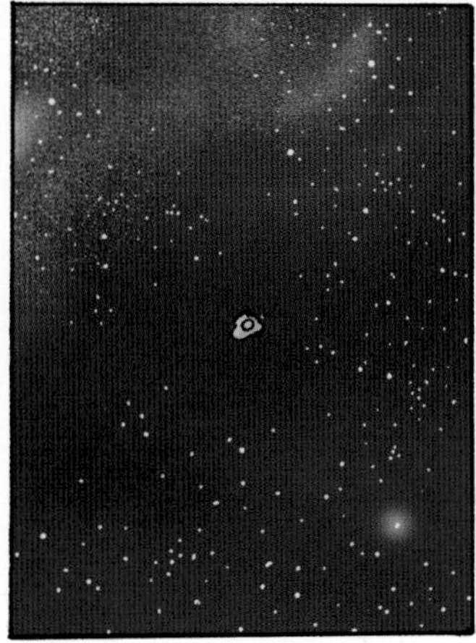

WINK!

FOOOSH!

MM?

MOUSE, WAKE UP! WE'RE HERE!

PSSH

HEY!

WADDLE IT BE, LADY?
REFUEL?
REPAIR?
TOP OFF THE FLUIDS?

TOUCH UP THE PAINT JOB?

WE'RE LOOKING FOR A SHIP WITH A GOLD AND BLUE DOME.
GOLD 'N' BLUE...

YOU MEAN PIPER'S SHIP!
YOU KNOW IT?

WELL SHOR 'IN I DO! HE TRAVELS WITH ZITA THE SPACEGIRL! SHE'S AWESOME!

SAAAY, YOU KINDA LOOK LIKE HER.
SHORTER MAYBE.
I-IS THE SHIP STILL HERE?

SHORE 'TIS! JES' TWO DOCKS OVER!
NUMMER FOUR!
THANKS.

HEH HEH. LOOKS JES' LIKE-
BREEP!

UHH.

DS
STOLEN VESSEL
SUSPECTS

ZITA!

GRAB A MOLTI!!

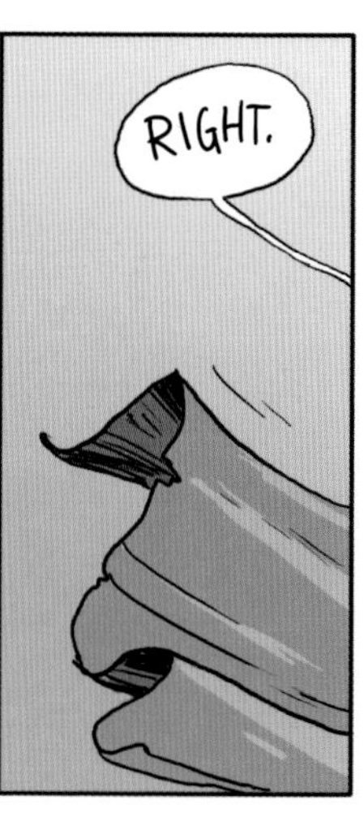
RIGHT.

THERE.

HEY!

SWISH!

THERE IT IS!

SHE WENT THIS WAY.

YOU SURE?

FAN OUT.

Ha Ha!

ONE MORE AUTOGRAPH AND THEN WE REALLY HAVE TO GO.

SKRITCH SCRATCH

BUCK!
SNAP!

GOT HER.
GRK!

SHE DON'T LOOK LIKE MUCH.
JUST BAG HER AN' TAG HER.

GRK!
P-PIPER!

?

HM.

GAH! SHE'S a FEISTY ONE!
HOLD'R STILL. I'LL TASER HER.

AAAH!

AUGH!
FOOMP!

GO MOUSE GO!

CHIEF? PRISONER IS LOOSE.
PRISONER IS LOOSE!

BOOK
DROP

WHOO.

ZITA THE SPACEGIRL-

HERO OR MENACE?

THE GIRL FROM PARTS UNKNOWN WHO ROCKETED TO FAME AFTER SHE SAVED PLANET SCRIPTORIUS FROM AN ASTEROID.

SEEN IN THIS SECURITY FEED HIJACKING A SPACECRAFT!

LET'S GET SOME OPINIONS!!

SHE WAS ONLY TRYING TO

EXPLODE US ALL!

THEY'RE EDITING THIS, JERRY.

BUSTED RIGHT OUT! I TELL YOU NO PRISON IN THE UNIVERSE CAN HOLD HER!

FILFY URCHIN STOLE THE CLOTHES OFFA M' BACK AN' RUINED M' BUSINESS AN STOLE AWAY ME BEST FRIEND!

'IS NAME WAS STRONG STRONG.

sniff.

are YOU SEEING THIS, MOUSE?
fooMP!

SKREEK!
MOUSE!

HISSs!

BAD CAT!
YOWRL!

YOU PUT HIM DOWN!

LEAP!
NO!

SLIP!
SPLOT

RGH.
DIDJA SEE THAT?

'AT'S HER INNIT?
IT IS! IT'S THAT HORRIBLE ZITA THE CRIMEGIRL!

-AN' SHE HAD THESE TERRIFYING LITTLE FLAT TEETH!

UH HUH, UH HUH.

GIBBIN' ME NIGHTMARES!

TRAMP
TRAMP
TRAMP

THERE!
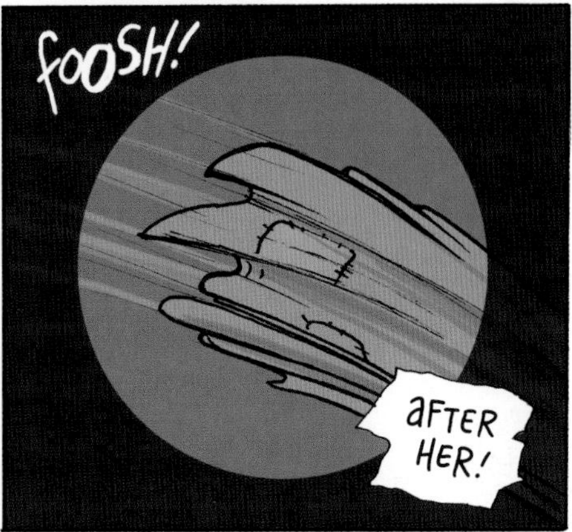
fOOSH!
AFTER HER!

SHE'S HEADING FOR THE DOME!

BRING IN THE AERIAL UNITS.

GASP!

FLOMP!

KAWK!
KAWK!

KRAWK!
RAWK
RAWK!
RAWK!

RAWK
RAWK
RAWK
AAH!

PECK
PECK
PECK

THIS LITTLE SQUIP SAVED A PLANET?

'S JUST RUMORS, STANLEY.

CAN IT, BOYS.

TIME TO SHUT THIS ONE DOWN FOR GOOD.

PAF!

HEY!
WHAT THE -
PSSSSSH!

CRACK!
WHAK
OOF!
THUMP
AUGH!
CRUNCH!

WHUMP

YOU MUST BE ZITA.

Chapter
Three

You!

KAWK KAWK

You NEED TO COME WITH ME.

How Do I KNOW I CaN TRUST YOU?
DON' TRUSTER!

You DON'T.
BUT I'M YOUR BEST CHANCE aT ESCaPING THIS PLaCE.
WE HaVE To HURRY.

I CaN'T.
MY FRIEND Was-
Was-
You MEaN YOUR "MOUSE"?

HE'S SaFE.

CHAK

BOOM

I DINNAE SEE NUFFIN!

KAWK!

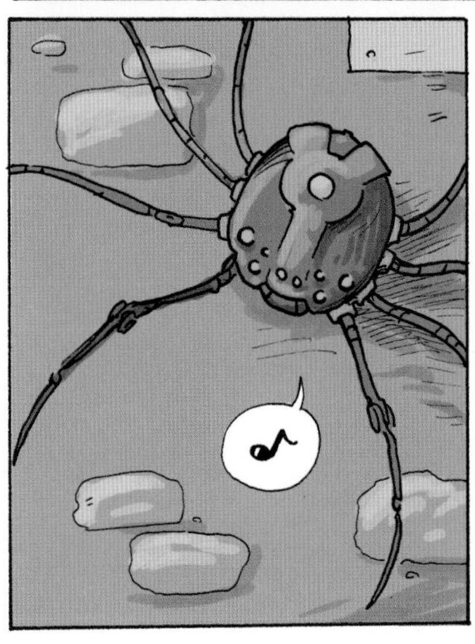

KEEP RUNNING! I'LL SLOW THEM DOWN!
?

KAK
KAW KAWK

BAP!
SQOOOSH!

POOM!
KAWK!

IT'S ANOTHER DEAD-

END?
SQOOOSH!

WAUGH!

SPRANG

POMF!

☹

STILTSKIN! GET THE ENGINES HUMMING!
WE'RE GOING TO NEED a QUICK EXIT.

THAT'S MY SHIP.

ZITa?

THOSE GUaRDS aRE RIGHT BEHIND US!

SWISH!

THERE THEY ARE!

IN OR OUT, ZITA.

FOOM!

WHEW.

CIRQUE
RUSTLE
DOP!

MOUSE!

GET away FROM HIM!

LISTEN, YOU-

AAAH!
PFFT!
PFFT!
COUGH!
PFFT!

HURK!
FLOMP!

flip
VIRTUE
STELLAR STORIES
A PATH TO BRAVERY
FAIRY TALES
THE HERO'S SACRIFICE

SH-SHE'S READ ONE HUNDRED AND FORTY-SEVEN BOOKS WITHOUT STOPPING.

AND SHE HASN'T BEEN PUTTING ORGANIC MATTER INTO HER SPEAKING APPARATUS.

eat?
YES! THAT.

SOMETHING IS AMISS.

YOU TWO, ALERT PIPER.

I WILL KEEP A VIGILANT EYE ON OUR SPACEGIRL.

THUMP
THUMP
SQUIGGa
SKWEE!

aHEM.

I'M BUSY.

BUT WE TH-THINK THERE'S S-SOMETHING WRONG WITH ZITa.

SO YOU'VE FIGURED IT OUT, HaVE YOU?
THaT THING IS NOT ZITa.

IT'S a ROBOT.

HMM...

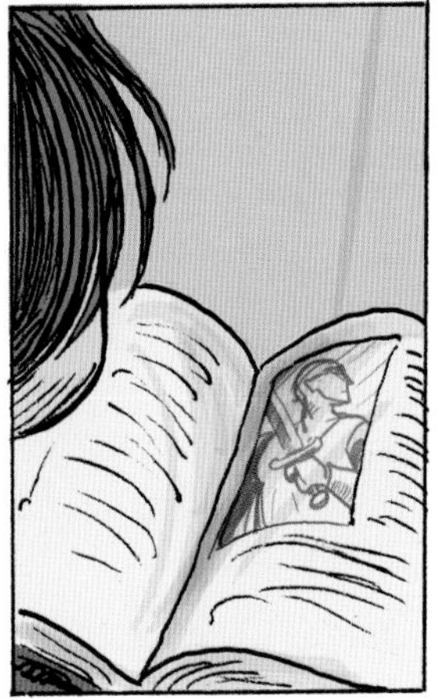

PERHAPS IT IS A
PHYSIOLOGICAL
PROBLEM...

WHAT??

IMPOSTOR! WHAT HAVE YOU DONE WITH ZITA?

FOOSH!

MOM!
DAD!

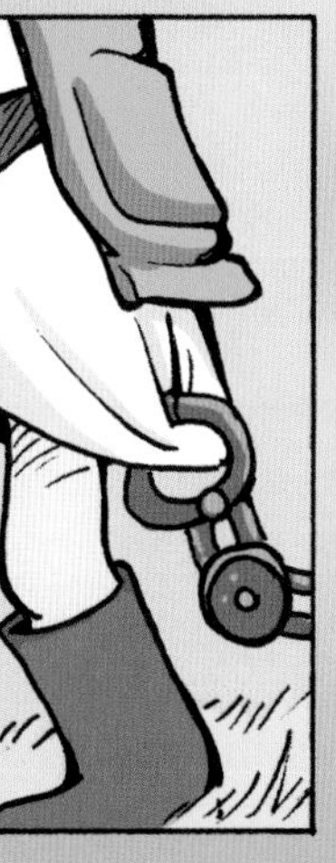

I CAN'T GO WITH YOU.
I BELONG HERE.
BUT-

ADVENTURES.

NOT FOR ME.

PLEASE!
YOU MUST!

LET ME GO!

THE
UNIVERSE
NEEDS
YOU!

HAVE SOME TEA.

IT'LL CLEAR YOUR HEAD.

I'M SORRY ABOUT STILTSKIN. THE GAS – IT'S A DEFENSE MECHANISM.
HE CAN'T HELP IT.
SIP.

HE'S A PRETTY DECENT MECHANIC THOUGH.

WHAT ABOUT MOUSE?

YOU MEAN PIZZICATO?
YES I KNOW HIS REAL NAME.

HE'S FINE. STILTSKIN WAS JUST CHECKING FOR INJURIES.

HOW DO YOU KNOW–

CREAK
CHOOM!!

THAT-
THAT SOUNDED KIND OF BAD.

DID THAT SOUND BAD TO YOU?

I'M AFRAID MY SHIP NEEDS SOME REPAIRS.

COME JOIN ME ON THE BRIDGE WHEN YOU'RE READY.
WE HAVE A LOT TO TALK ABOUT.

GULP.

sniff

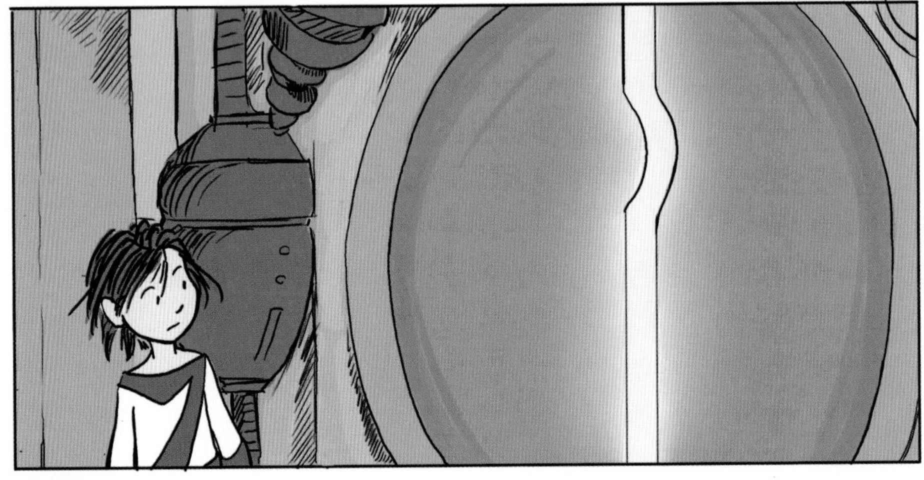

SCOOTCH

GILLIAM'S GUIDE

SCUFFLE

I TELL Ya, BOYS -

THIS OPERATION'S FALLIN' APART AT THE SEAMS.
I CAN KEEP PATCHIN' THE ENGINE TOGETHER
BUT THIS SHIP NEEDS NEW PARTS.

ZUB ZUFFIN GLONK.
WELL IT AIN'T MY FAULT!

THE SHOWS AIN'T PULLIN' IN HALF WHAT THEY USED TO.
AN' NOW WE GOT THE MISTRESS TAKIN' IN STRAYS.

MARK MY WORDS: THAT GIRL AN' HER RODENT ARE TROUBLE.
WE OUGHTA TOSS 'EM OUT THE AIRLOCK.
DOP!
POP!

DOP, DOP DOPPLE DOP!

NOW DON'T YOU START MORALIZIN' AT ME, DOPPELGANGER!

BAH! YOU TWO GOT NO IMAGINATION.

BUT THINGS ARE DUE FOR A CHANGE AROUND HERE.

GLISSANDO
LAP
LAP
LAP!

PRRRRR.
Z

THERE ARE STORIES ABOUT YOU.

FIRST I HEARD YOU WERE SOME KIND OF WANDERING HERO,
OFF TO SAVE ANOTHER PLANET.

THEN THERE WERE REPORTS THAT YOU WERE A DANGEROUS CRIMINAL.
DOOM SQUAD ON YOUR TRAIL AND EVERYTHING.

NOW THERE'S A REWARD.
PIZZICATO THE PLUNDERER
ZITA THE CRIME GIRL
ARTISTS DEPICTION
BIG REWARD

IT COULD BE TROUBLE.

ARE YOU GOING TO TURN ME IN?

YOU'RE NO CRIMINAL.

CLICK

YOU THINK I'M A HERO.

I THINK YOU'RE LIKE THE REST OF US.

PLIP!
JUST TRYING TO HOLD THINGS TOGETHER WHILE YOU FIND YOUR WAY.

BUT I ALSO THINK THE ROLE SUITS YOU.

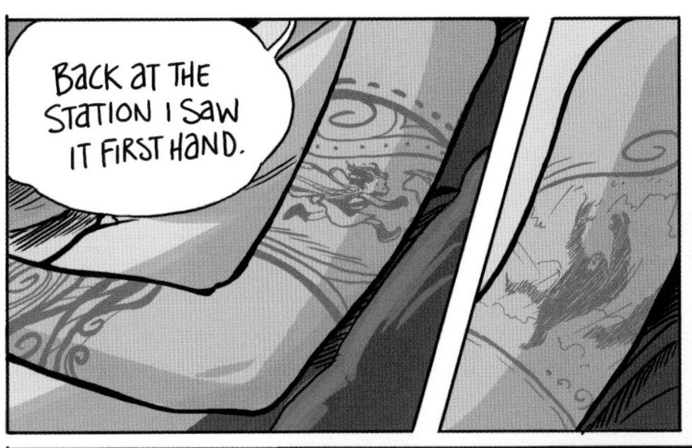
Back at the station I saw it first hand.

You shine in a crisis.

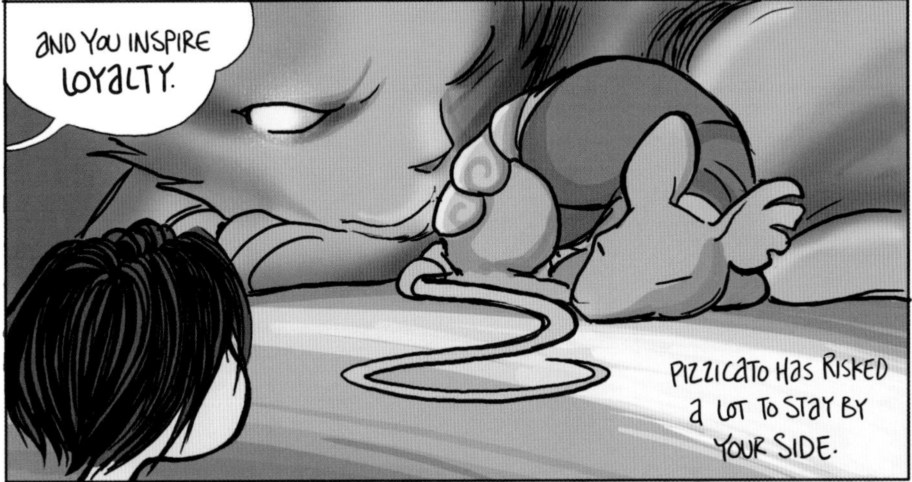
And you inspire loyalty.
Pizzicato has risked a lot to stay by your side.

This isn't his first brush with the law you know.

They were outlaws.
Quite the team until they were separated.

THAT'S WHY YOU GAVE ME TICKETS TO YOUR SHOW? BECAUSE YOU SAW MOUSE?
THAT'S RIGHT.

BUT THAT'S NOT THE ONLY REASON, IS IT?

WHAT DO YOU MEAN?
POOF!

I KNOW YOU USED TO TRAVEL WITH PIPER.

ZITA...

BOOM!

THAT WASN'T ENGINE FAILURE.

THAT WAS ANOTHER SHIP.

DOOM SQUAD! OPEN UP!

BOOM
HIT IT AGAIN. BREAK IT DOWN!

YOU!

YOU TALKED ALL ABOUT BEING A HERO AND YOU TURNED ME IN TO FIX YOUR SHIP!
ZITA-

CHOOM!
GET DOWN!

HSSS!

LET GO OF ME, TRAITOR!
I KNOW ALL ABOUT YOU AND PIPER AND YOU'RE JUST THE SAME!

END OF THE ROAD, SCUMBAGS.

WE BROUGHT THE BIG GUNS.

STOP!
eh?

I WANT MY REWARD.

HEH.
SHRINKEY...

CHAK
GIVE THE MANNIKIN HIS REWARD.

FZOT!

SHRINK!

DOP?

MADRIGAL, I-
NO TIME FOR THAT. WE'VE GOT TO GET YOU TO THE ESCAPE POD!

YOWR!

GLISSANDO, NO!

FZOT!
FOMF!
GRRR...

POP!

POP! POP!
WHAT THE-?
POP! POP! POP!
POP POP! POP
POP POP
POP!
HE'S MULTIPLYIN', CHIEF!

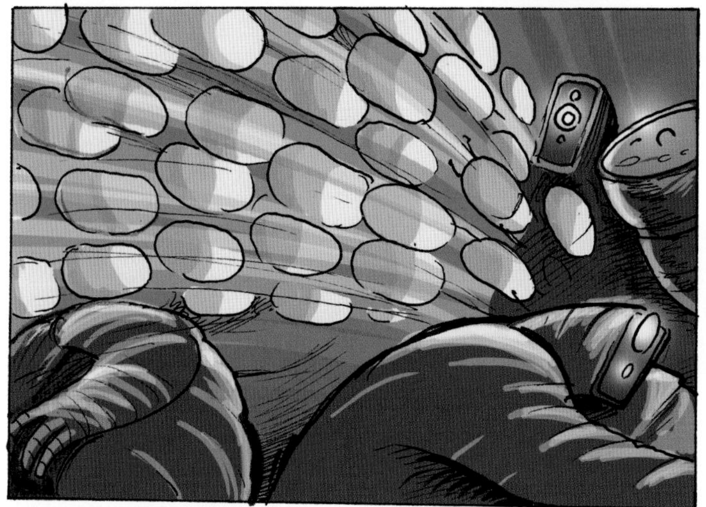

FSSSSS
DOP.

BOOM!

ZITA, PLEASE! WE CAN'T HOLD THEM OFF FOR LONG!
WAIT!

MOUSE!

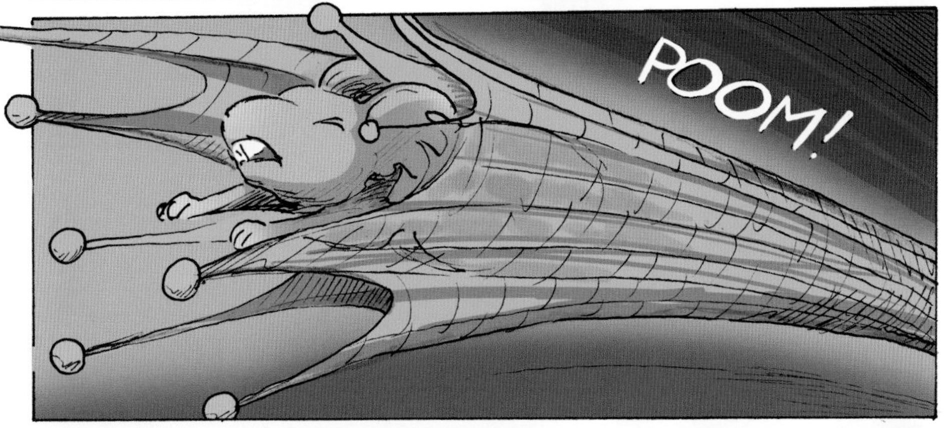
POOM!

Ha.

GOT 'IM.

THEY'VE GOT MOUSE!

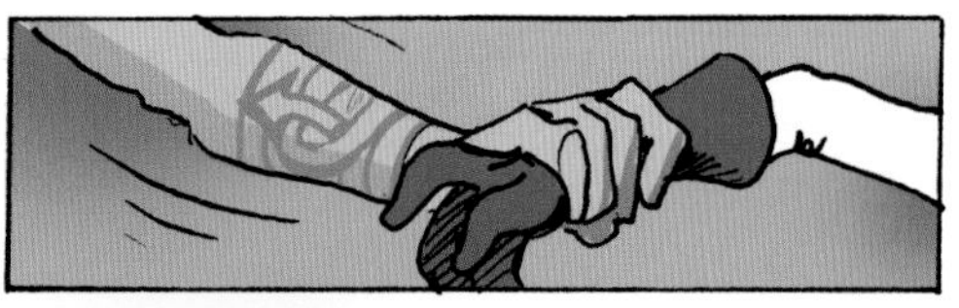

AND IF THEY CATCH YOU TOO THEN YOUR JOURNEY IS OVER!
LET GO!

CHING!
GO!

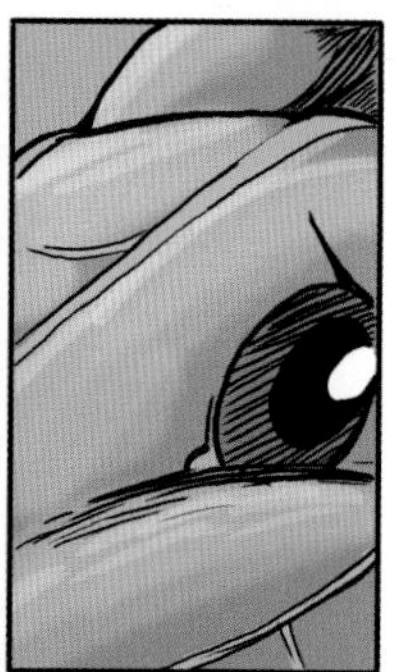

I'LL COME FIND YOU, MOUSE!

I PROMISE

CLOMP CLOMP CLOMP!

SHOVE!

GIVE THIS TO PIPER.

SHOOM!

RINGMISTRESS.

STEP AWAY FROM THE POD.

EJECT!

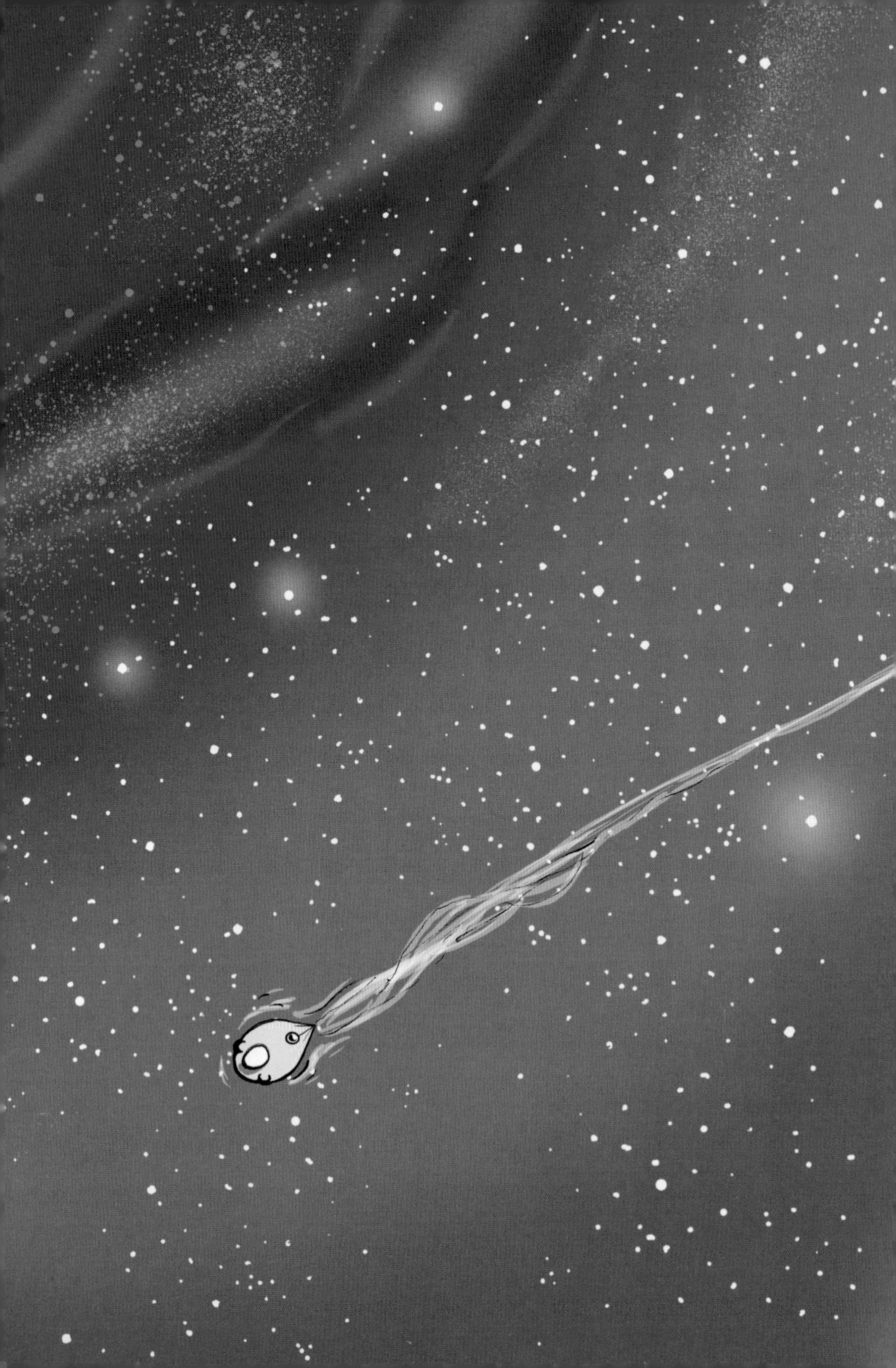

MROW?

LISTEN CLOSELY.

IF YOU ARE RECEIVING THIS, THEN I'VE GIVEN YOU THE POD AHEAD OF SCHEDULE.
THERE ARE THINGS YOU SHOULD KNOW.
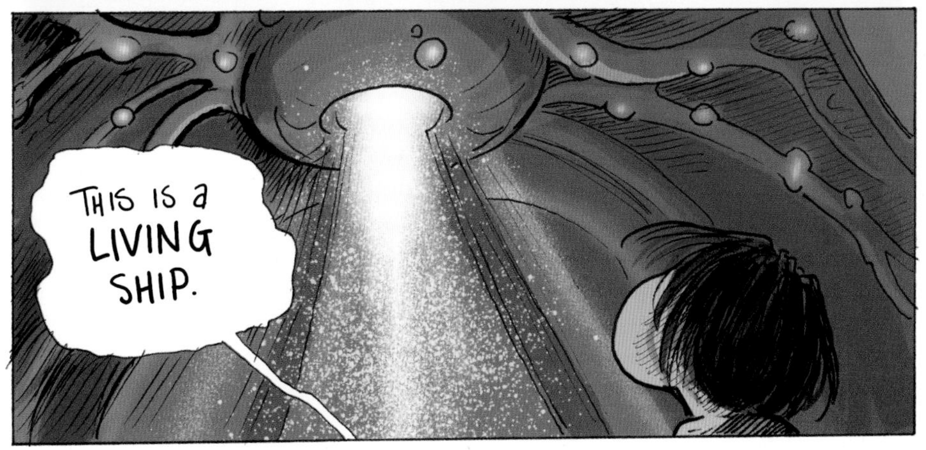
THIS IS A LIVING SHIP.

SHE CAN'T YET FLY ON HER OWN...
YOU NEED TO ESTABLISH A MENTAL CONNECTION WITH THE SHIP. WAKE HER UP AND SHE WILL TAKE YOU WHEREVER YOU NEED TO GO.

SHE'S YOURS, ZITA.

GUIDE HER WELL.

PING

Chapter
Four

IT TOOK ME a WHILE TO FIGURE IT OUT.

NOT MaNY BOTS COULD PULL OFF a MIMIC LIKE THaT.

repli-
anoid
riety of
cles.
pera-
us

st worlds.

T-BOT
3rd generation
ockwork

Imprint-o-Tron (holo-bot prototype)

Designed to mimic the appearance and behavior of a variety of organic species and built for companionship, the Imprint-o-Tron was deemed a danger to society due to a tendency to fixate on individuals being mimicked to the point that a few of the robots attempted to "replace" their targets.

After the OmniDroid Recall and the subsequent tragedy known as the Great Dismantling, it is believed that none of the holo-bot prototypes remain in existence.

WH-WHAT DO WE DO?
I NEED TO THINK.
IT MUST HAVE STRANDED ZITA SOMEWHERE.
NOW IT'S LOOSE ON THE SHIP AND-

PING

AND IT SEEMS TO HAVE DEFEATED ONE!

SHUFFLE

C-CAN YOU M-MAKE HER DANCE?
IT'S STILL a ROBOT.
MY MUSIC WON'T AFFECT IT.

STEP

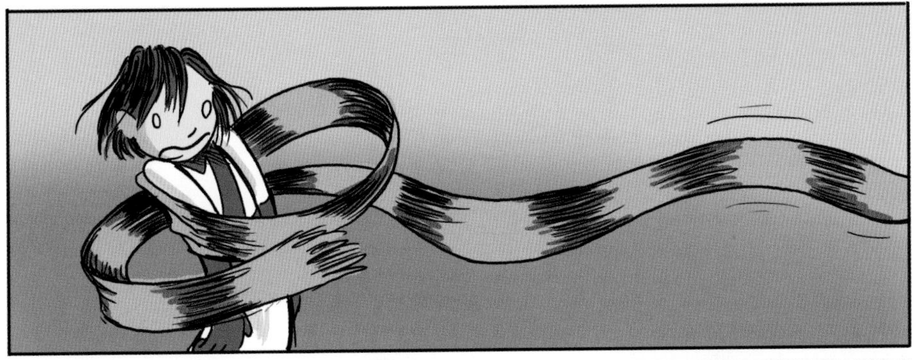

CAREFUL. IT ONLY GETS TIGHTER IF YOU STRUGGLE.
So GLAD I LEARNED TO KNIT.

NOW DON'T MAKE TROUBLE.

whistle MAN?

"PIPER!" MY NAME IS "PIPER."

HOW MANY TIMES DO I HAVE TO-
OH.

HIS INITIALIZER IS FRIED BUT HIS SYSTEM SHOULD REBOOT.

NO PERMANENT DAMAGE.

P-P-PIPER?

WE'RE APPROACHING
A P-PLANET.

BLING!

YOU MADE IT!
WE KNEW YOU'D SAVE US!

WELCOME TO LUMPONIA!

LOOK, I'M SORRY BUT WE CAN'T HELP YOU.
W-WHAT?

BUT ZITA THE SPACEGIRL!
SHE-

SHE PROMISED!

THAT'S THE THING, SEE... WE SORT OF...
LOST HER.

GONE? THE HERO OF LUMPONIA IS -MISSING?

AH! AH HA! YOU JOKE WITH US!
YOU BRING THE LIGHT OF HUMOR TO OUR DARKEST HOUR!
WHAT? NO!

I MEAN IT- WE WILL NOT BE LANDING ON YOUR PLANET!
CHZZT!

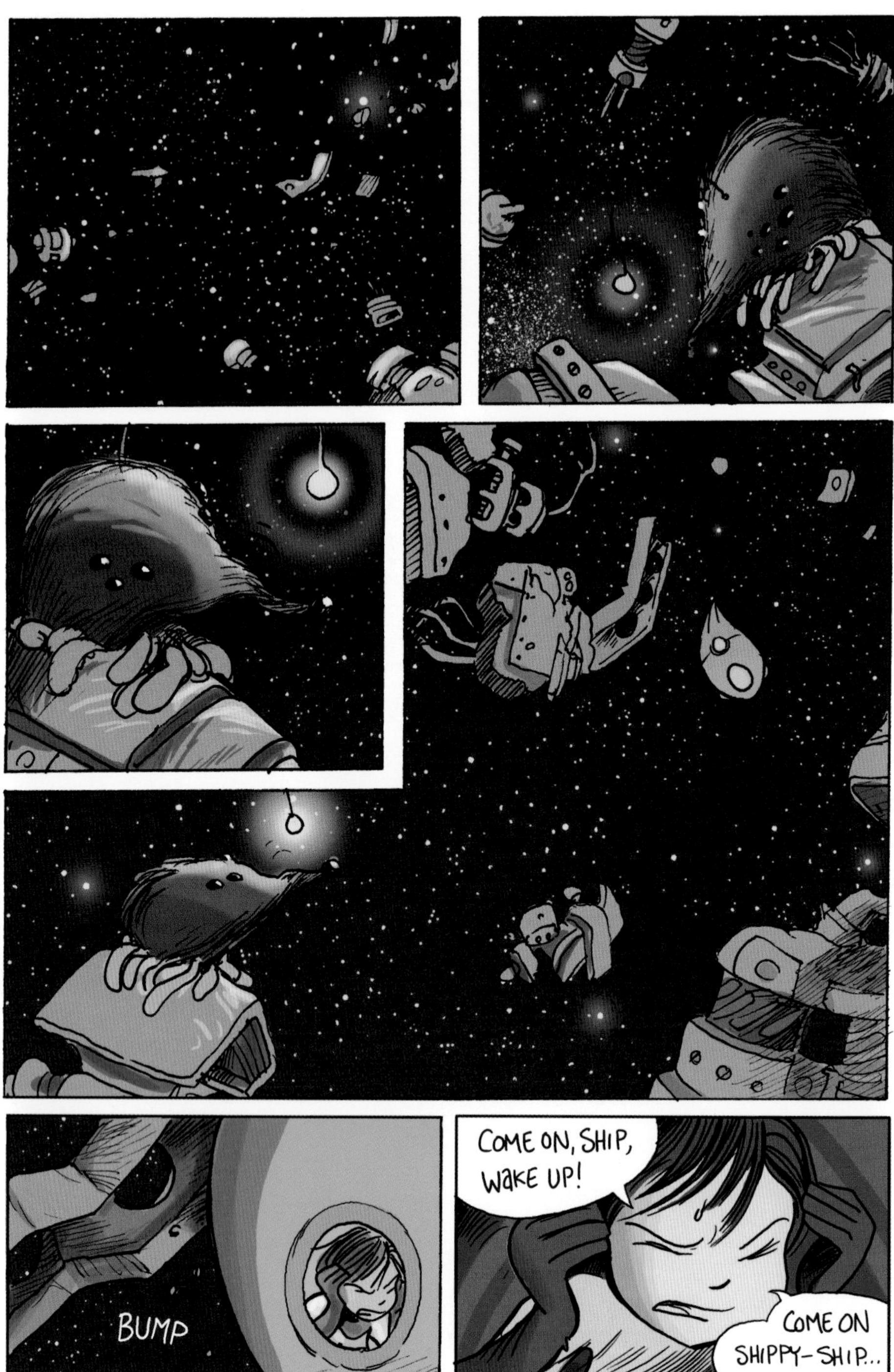
BUMP
COME ON, SHIP, WAKE UP!
COME ON SHIPPY-SHIP...

COME ON, SHIPPY...

THIS ISN'T WORKING.

YEAH? WELL NO ONE ASKED YOU TO COME!
THANKS TO YOU I'LL NEVER SEE MY FRIENDS OR MY HOME AGAIN!

OH-

HEY. COME ON. DON'T CRY.
LOOK IT'S JUST- I'VE NEVER HAD TO WAKE UP A SPACESHIP WITH MY BRAIN BEFORE SO-

OW!
BITE!

HEY-

I THINK I KNOW THAT GUY.

FLASH
FLASH
FLASH!

CAN YOU HELP US? WE'RE TRYING TO REACH LUMPONIA.

FOOSH!

I GUESS THAT'S A **NO.**

CHUNK!

CLINK CHANK!
CRiiiRK.

VROT!

TEMPORARY ENGINES?
THANK YOU!
ZITA!

WE'RE ALMOST THERE.
I CAN EVEN TRACK WHERE THEY LANDED.

THIS SHIP IS AMAZING!
TUG TUG

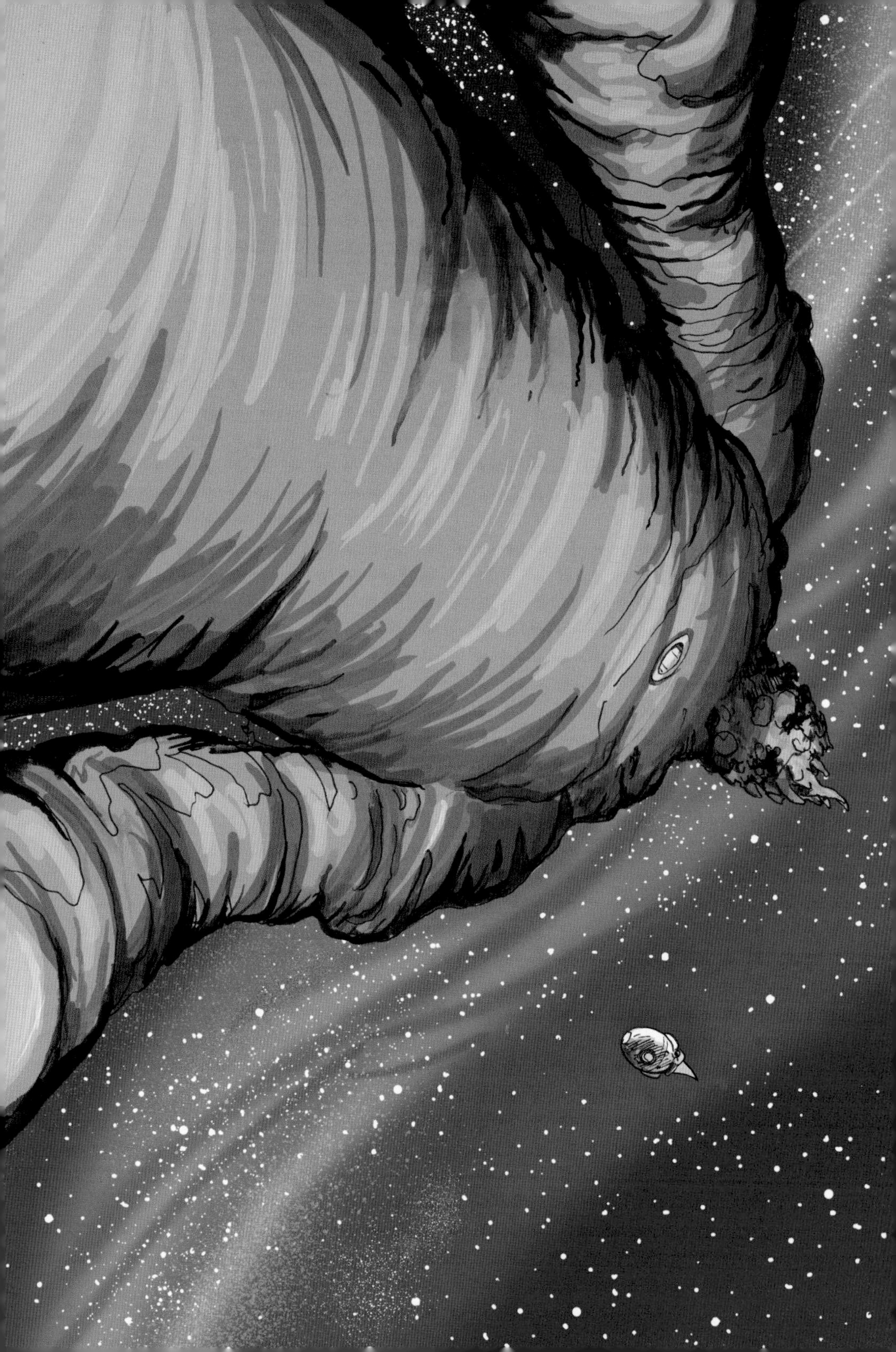

IT'S NOT MOVING.

MAYBE IT'S ASLEEP.

OR DEAD.

landing sequence

MEW

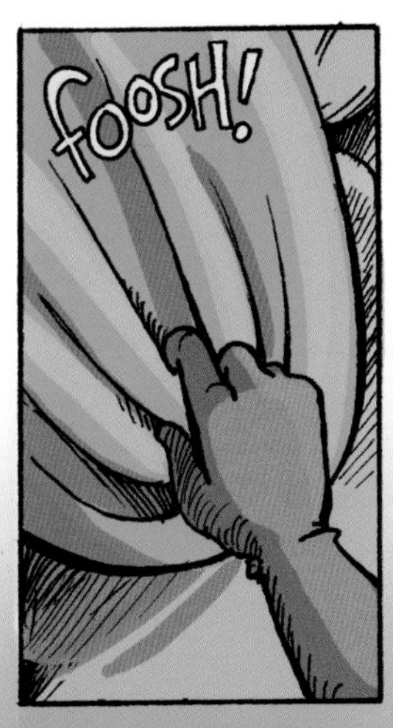
FOOSH!

READY?

SCUFFLE

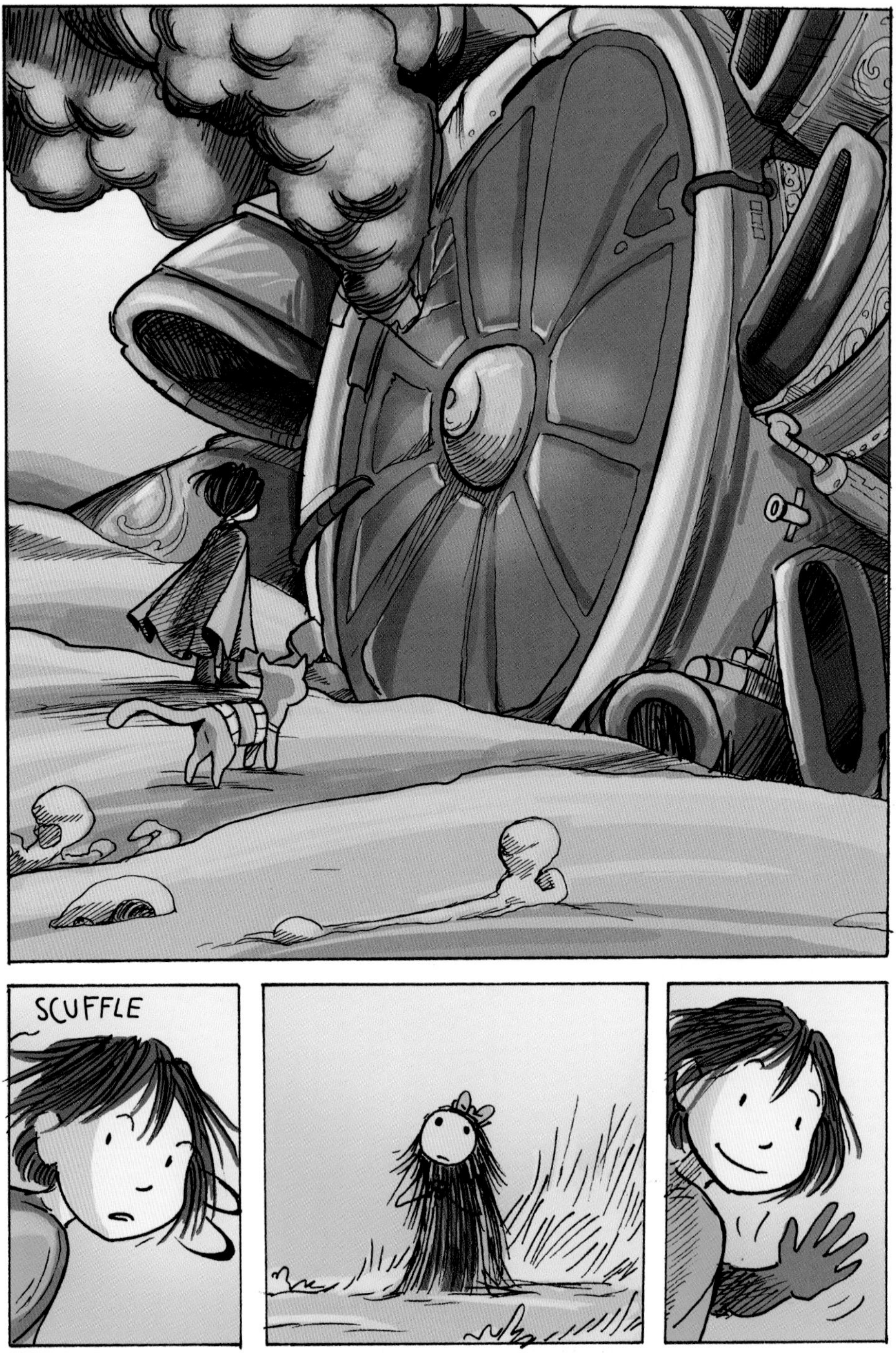

HI THERE.
DID YOU SEE WHERE THE PEOPLE FROM THAT SHIP WENT?

SCREEACH!
SHOOM!

WHAT ARE THOSE-

-THINGS?

LET US GO!
PIPER?

YOU CAN'T DO THIS!

YOU NEED TO EVACUATE THIS PLANET BEFORE THOSE STAR HEARTS ARRIVE!

BUT WE HAVE ZITA THE SPACEGIRL NOW!
NO THANKS TO YOU!

THAT'S WHAT I'M TRYING TO TELL YOU!
YOU'VE GOT THE WRONG ZITA!

NONSENSE! LOOK HOW HEROIC SHE IS!

SEE?

THAT'S IT.

POW!
GIVE ME BACK MY LIFE!

I AM ZITA!
OH NO YOU'RE NOT!

lost girl?

hnh.
STRAIN!
VVT!
THERE'S TWO OF 'EM!

TWO ZITAS?!?
OH, OH! THE SHORT ONE MUST BE HER STUNT DOUBLE!
YEAH? WELL WADDLE I DO WIT' 'EM?
SEND THEM BOTH!
SEND US BOTH? SEND US BOTH WHERE?!?
TO THE GIANT, OF COURSE!

IT WAS LEFT HERE AGES AGO TO PROTECT THIS WORLD.
BUT ONLY A TRUE HERO CAN CONTROL IT.
THERE'S NO ONE LIKE THAT ON THIS PLANET.

RRRR...
snap!
snap
snap!
THAT'S
DOUBLE REINFORCED
RESTRAINIUM!
YOU REALLY
ARE STRONG
STRONG.
Snap!
SCREEEE!
WE'RE
TOO
LATE!

HEART ATTACK!
SNAP!

RAWR!

CLICK

SIGH.
I AM GOOD...

ZITA!

I THINK I CAN FREE YOU BEFORE THE OTHER HEARTS ARRIVE.

NO.
WHAT?

LAUNCH US.

ZITA-
DO IT!
BEFORE I CHICKEN OUT!

SHOOMP!

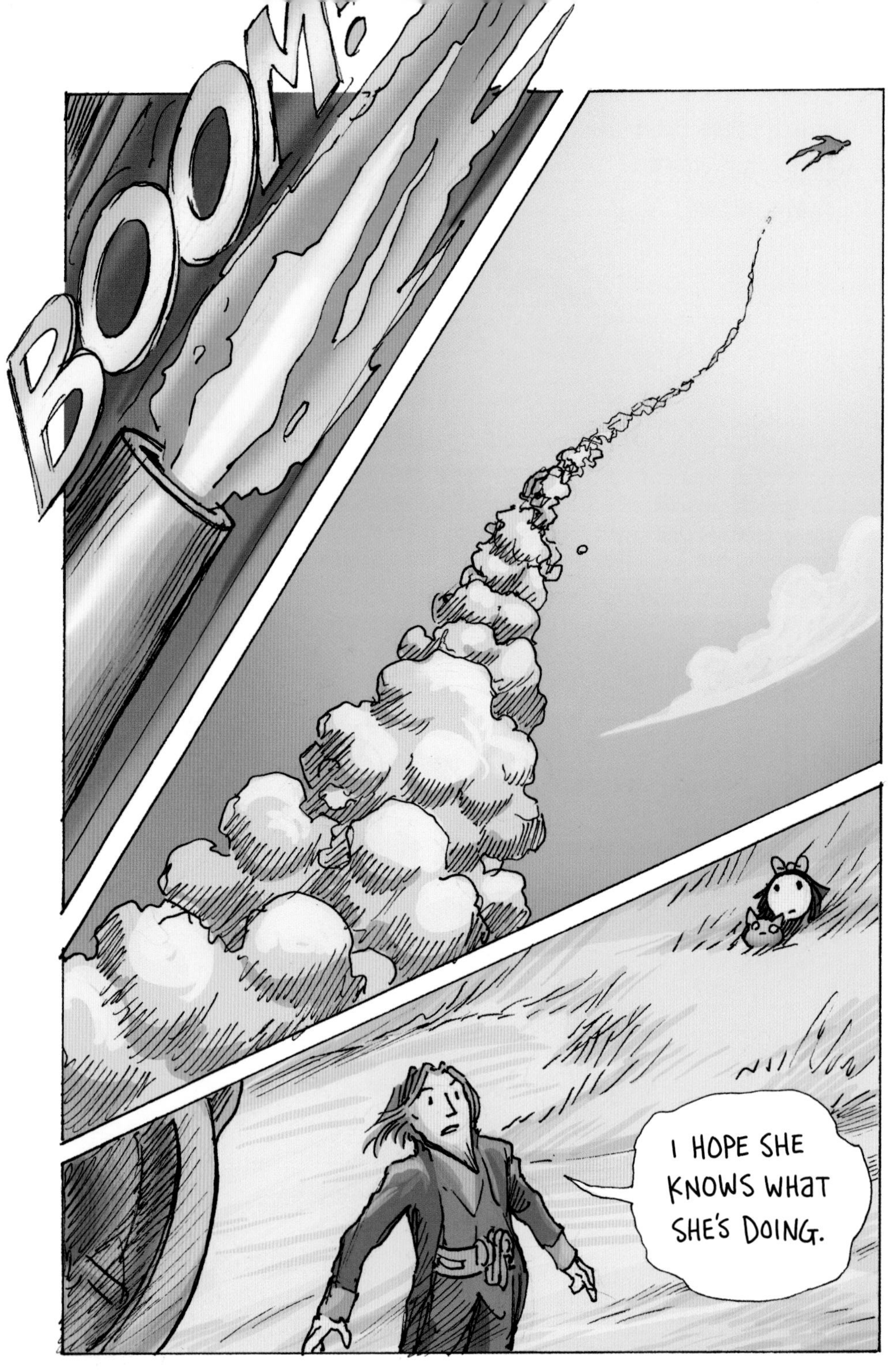
BOOOM!
I HOPE SHE KNOWS WHAT SHE'S DOING.

Chapter
Five

I HAVE NO IDEA WHAT I'M DOING.

STOP IT! YOU ARE NOT ME!
I AM ZITA!

LET'S NOT MAKE ANY MORE SUDDEN MOVEMENTS.

SO MANY OF THEM.
WHY HAVEN'T THEY ATTACKED THE PLANET YET?

THEY WAIT FOR THEIR QUEEN.
THEIR WHAT?

tar Hearts
rstellar scavengers
capable of unassisted
spaceflight, star hearts
are the scourge of many
a planetary system.
Star Heart Swarms consist of several thousand
drones all under the command of a single
"queen." Swarms attack a planet and, after
consuming all organic matter, remain on
the planet's surface to reproduce.
After a gestation period a new, larger swar
d returns to space in search
supporting planet.

YOU MEMORIZED ALL THAT?
THAT'S-

THAT'S KIND OF AMAZING.

RRRRRRR.
UH OH.
WE'VE BEEN SPOTTED.

SNAP!

WE MADE IT.

WE MADE IT!!
HIGH FIVE!

NOW YOU PUT YOUR HAND UP.

SMEK!

COME ON.
SMEK SMEK

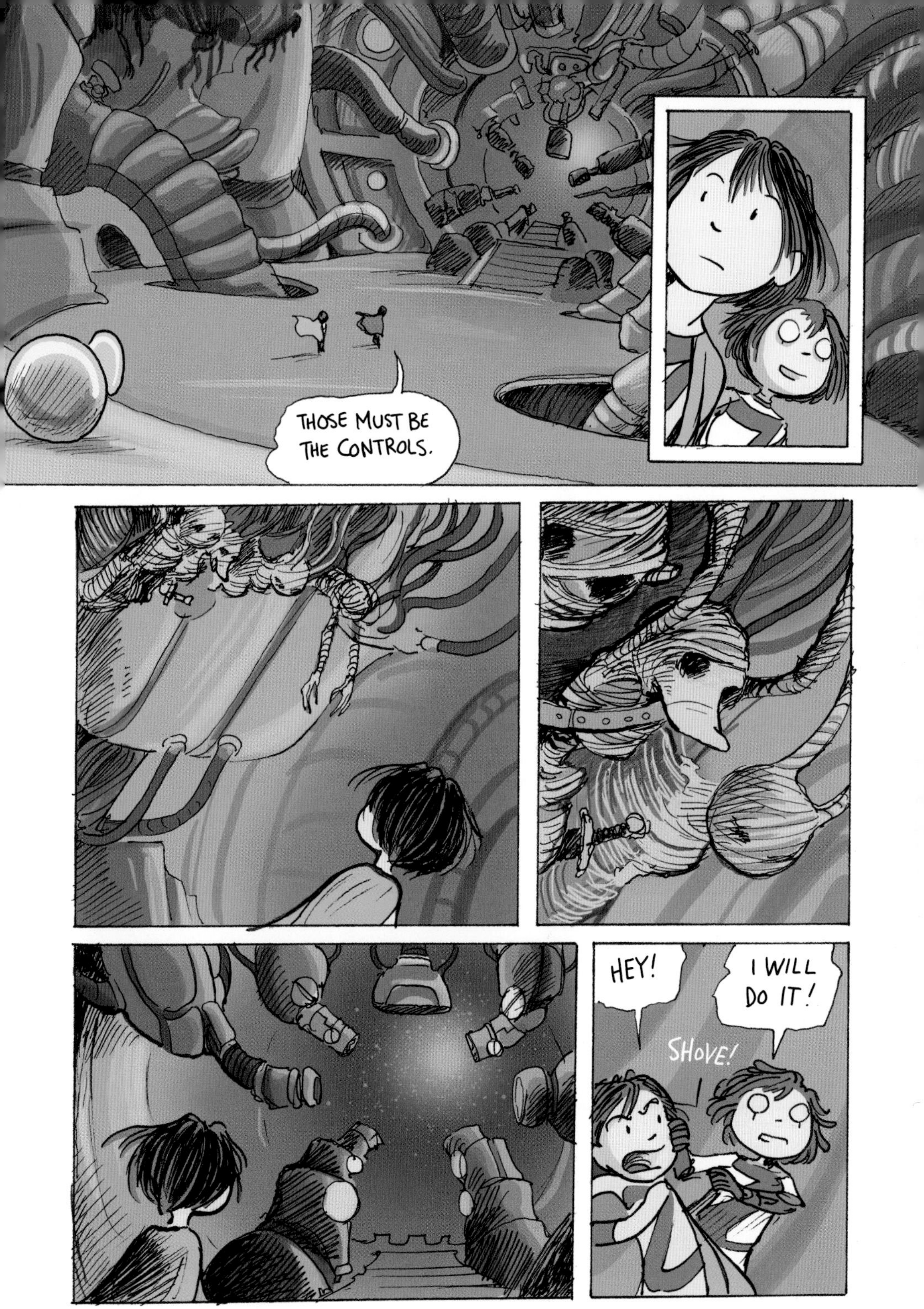

THOSE MUST BE THE CONTROLS.

THEY SAID THE GIANT WOULD ONLY RESPOND TO A "TRUE HERO."

I DON'T THINK WE'LL BE ABLE TO
AAH!

IT DOESN'T WANT ME.

IT WANTS YOU.
YOU'RE THE HERO.

CHAK
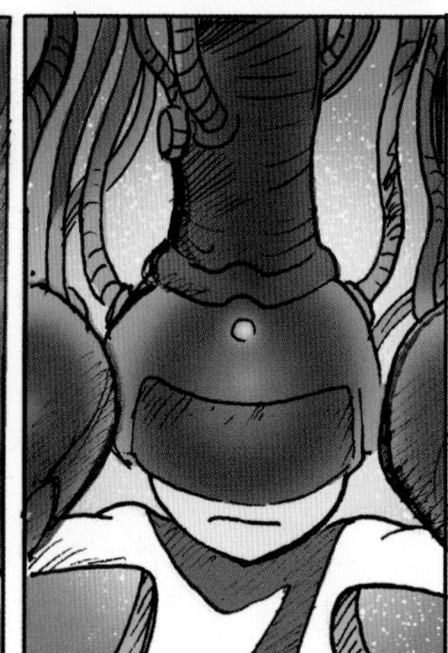

WOW!

SCREEEEEE!

NOT SO FAST, QUEEN.
LEAVE THAT PLANET ALONE!

SCREEK!

IT IS a CHALLENGE TO BATTLE.
WHAT? HOW DO YOU KNOW THAT?

GILLIAM'S INTRODUCTORY TO DEEP SPACE DIALECTS.
PAGE 427.
IT STATES-
OKAY OKAY!

CHALLENGE ACCEPTED!

BOOM!
NH! SHE'S STRONG!
SKREE!
HA!

BLIP
BLIP

PING!

READY FOR BATTLE!

BOOOOOM!
OOOH!

KA-BOOM!
AAAHH!

I SEEM TO HAVE MISSED SOMETHING.
ZITA'S USING A GIANT THE SIZE OF A TINY MOON TO BATTLE THE STAR HEARTS
-AND WINNING.

I MISS
ALL THE FUN.

THINK OF THE
POWER!

I DOUBT YOU WOULD
HAVE BEEN ABLE TO
UNLOCK THE CONTROLS.

THE HERO-LOCK MEANS
THE GIANT ONLY RESPONDS
TO SOMEONE WHO IS
WILLING TO-
TO...

OH
NO!

WHAT A BATTLE!
I KNEW SHE WAS THE ONE!

WHU-
GUH.

FLOMP!

URK!

WHERE IS IT? WHERE'S THE JUMP CRYSTAL YOU PROMISED HER?
I-I CAN'T I-D-DON'T-

YOU DON'T HAVE IT DO YOU?
BECAUSE YOU DIDN'T EXPECT HER TO COME BACK.

TELL ME WHAT'S HAPPENING TO HER!
WHOEVER PILOTS THE GIANT IS CONSUMED BY IT!

THEY CONTROL IT UNTIL DEATH.

ONE! YOU'VE GOT TO WARN ZITA!

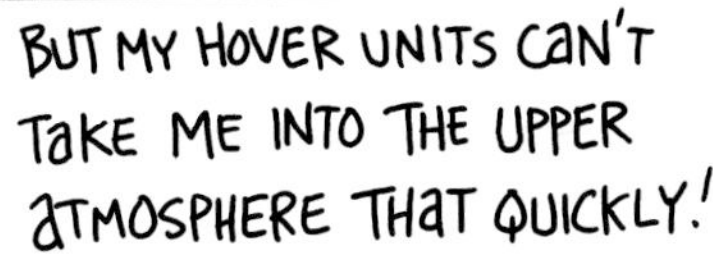
BUT MY HOVER UNITS CAN'T TAKE ME INTO THE UPPER ATMOSPHERE THAT QUICKLY!

NOT WITHOUT SOME KIND OF BOOST.

ONE?
ALMOST THERE-

SHOOM!
ZITA!
PIPER SENT ME TO WARN YOU THAT-
NO!

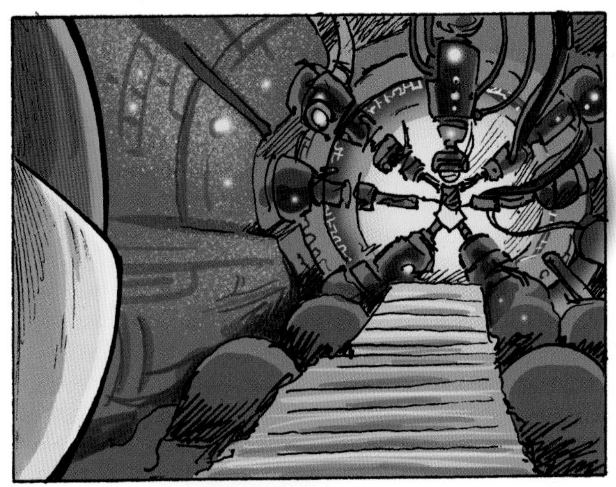

PIPER-
I AM TOO LATE.

THEN I WAS RIGHT.

THE LOCK IS BASED ON SELF-SACRIFICE
SHE'S MERGING WITH THE GIANT.
IF YOU PULL HER OUT NOW IT WILL SHUT DOWN AND NOTHING WILL STOP THOSE HEARTS.
BUT IF SHE STAYS CONNECTED-

WE'VE LOST HER.

NO.

YOU!
DO NOT FIRE.
KA CHAK!

THERE IS A REASON I SHOULD NOT REDUCE YOU TO SCRAP AND ASH?

PULL TRUE ZITA FREE.

I WILL TAKE HER PLACE.

BOOOM!
WHAT'S HAPPENING UP THERE, ONE?

BA DOOM!
THE GIANT'S GETTING POUNDED!

NOT NOW, WHISTLE MAN!
WE ARE BUSY.

WHISTLE MAN!

CRACK

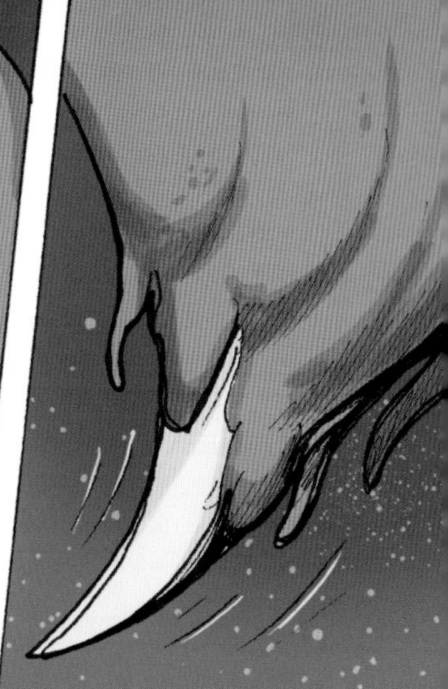

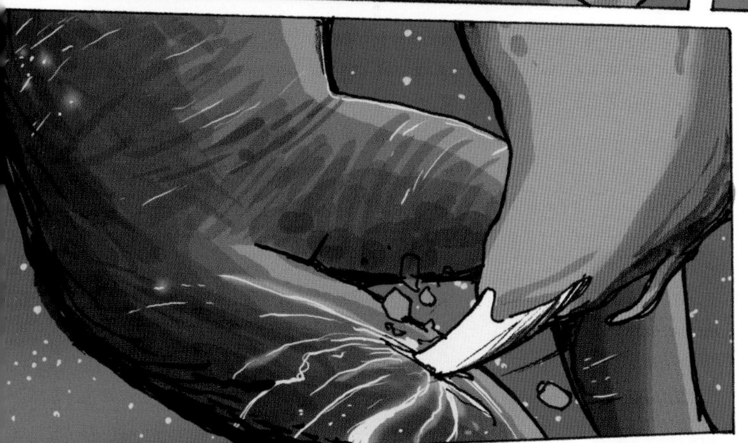

AAH!

STAND ASIDE!
VVT!

SNAP!
VVVVT!
SNAP!
SNAP!

BOOM!

RUMBLE!

THE GIANT...
IT WAS GOING TO-NH!
KEEP ME.

CHAK

NO!

YOU'LL BECOME PART OF IT! FOREVER!

I WILL BE A HERO
FOR YOU.
FOR THE LUMPIES.

WE MUST MAKE A TACTICAL RETREAT!
LET GO!
SMEK!

UNH!

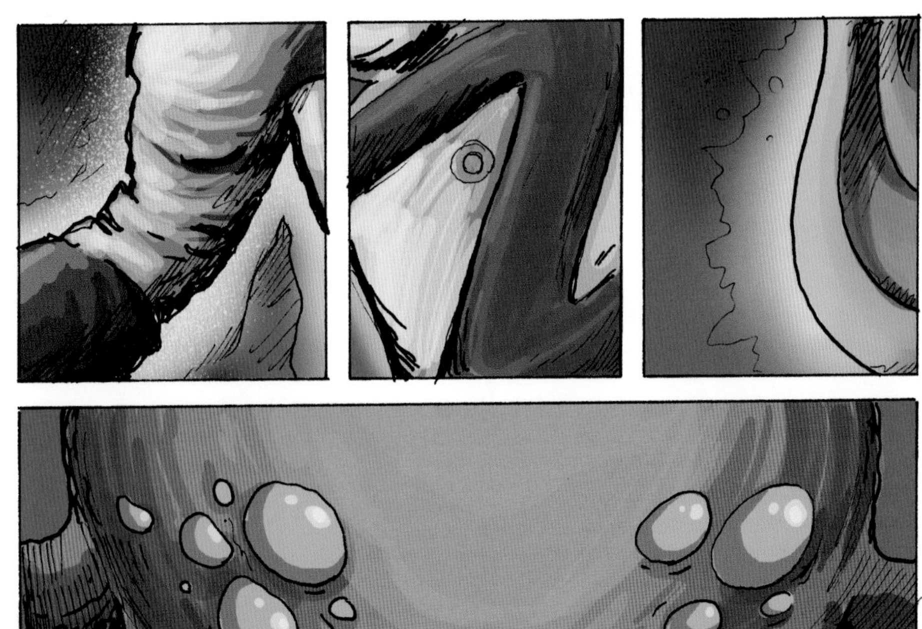

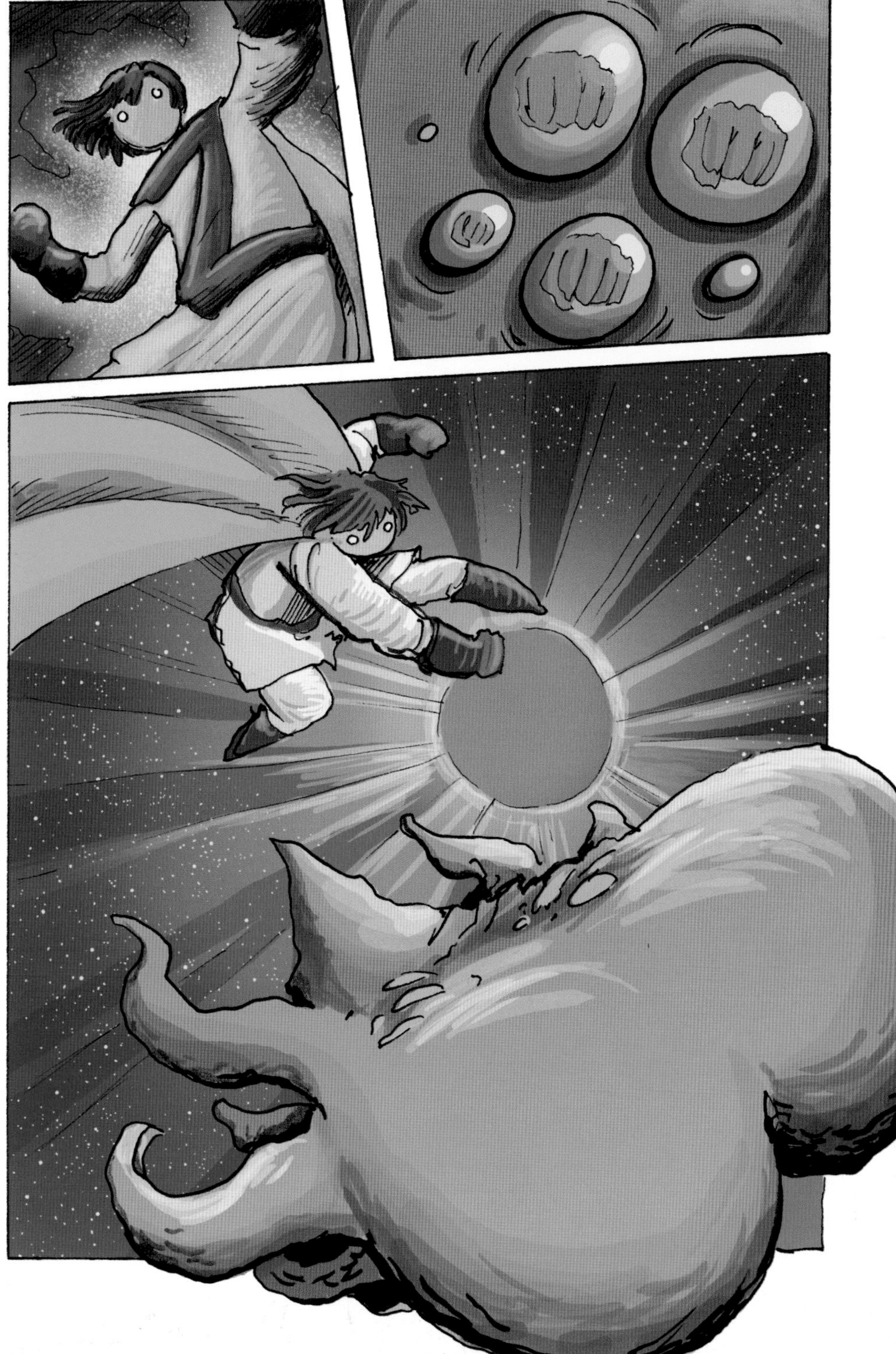

SHE DID IT!
THE HEARTS ARE RETREATING!
ZITA!

SHE DID IT.
ONE! DID YOU SEE?
ROBOT ZITA DID IT! SHE-
CRACK

ONE, WAKE UP!
WAKE UP!

CHNK!

SHIPPY...

CRINK

SHIPPY!
PLEASE WAKE UP!
SHLP!

FOSH!

FOOSH

Chapter
Six

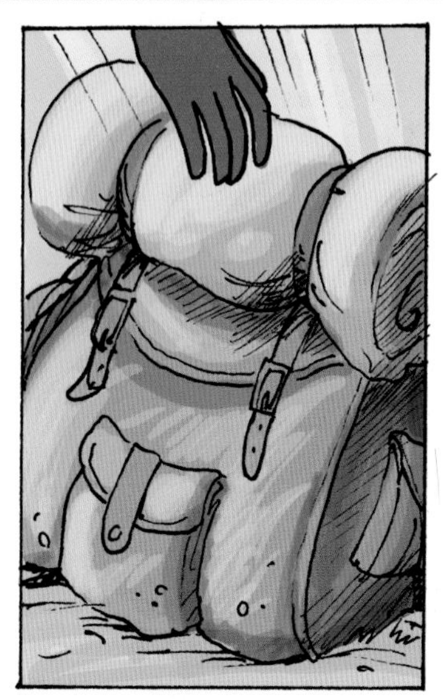

AHEM.

MAYBE NOT THE BEST WAY TO STOP THE LEGEND FROM GROWING.

MM?

OH.

SO I TURNED INTO A GIANT. MAYBE PEOPLE WILL ASSUME THIS IS HOW THE STORY ENDS.
HEH.
WE'LL SEE.

SO.
YOU'RE SURE ABOUT THIS?

MOUSE IS IN TROUBLE AND IT'S MY FAULT. I HAVE TO GO AFTER HIM.
AND YOUR SHIP WON'T BE FIXED FOR WEEKS.

BESIDES,

MAYBE IT'S TIME I TRAVELED ON MY OWN FOR A WHILE.

SO. SPEAKING OF TRAVEL-

CATCH.

THEY NEVER HAD A CRYSTAL AT ALL
BUT MAYBE YOU'LL FIND ONE OUT THERE.

MROW!
I'M READY.

THAT CAT-!
HIS NAME IS GLISSANDO.
MROW!

M-MADRIGAL'S CAT? Y-YOU MET MADRIGAL?

OH!
SHE WANTED ME TO GIVE YOU SOMETHING.

OH BOY.
GULP.
SLAP!
PIPER, I DIDN'T KNOW-
IT'S OKAY.
I KIND OF DESERVED THAT.

SIGH.

SNIFF!

WE'RE ≡NNH!≡ COMING WITH YOU!
SCOOCH!

TO PROTECT YOU!

THERE'S NO ROOM FOR YOU IN MY SHIP.
AND YOU NEED TIME FOR REPAIRS.

SHLP!

YOU'LL CATCH UP TO ME SOON.

SMEK.

ADMIT ONE
ADMIT ONE
ARE YOU READY?

MROW!
CLIK
RIGHT.

LET'S GO SAVE OUR FRIEND.

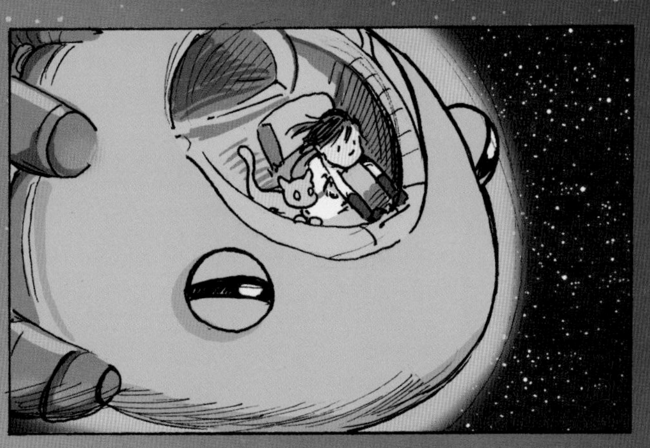

ATTENTION VESSEL!
CUT THRUSTERS and STAY WHERE YOU are!

TO BE CONTINUED . . .

SKETCHES

OH I CAN DO WHATEVER I SET MY MIND TO!!
MY HOBBY IS CASTING WITHERING GLANCES.
DO NOT KISS THE COOK
'ZIT TRUE YOU PUNCH'D A HOLE THRU TIME ISSELF?

I FLOAT BECAUSE I AM LIGHT HEARTED.
NOW I JES' NEED A HET.
I'M BETTER'N YOU! I'M BETTER'N YOU!
SPROINKA SPROINKA
CHENKA CHENKA
PUT ME IN YOUR BOOK!
NOW YOU MUST DEFEAT ME IN SINGLE COMBAT!
I'M NOT GOING TO FIGHT A PUPPET.

Madrigal

Z.
YOU CAN.
all
HERO.
YOU'LL VISIT MY
PLANET NEXT.
DOP.

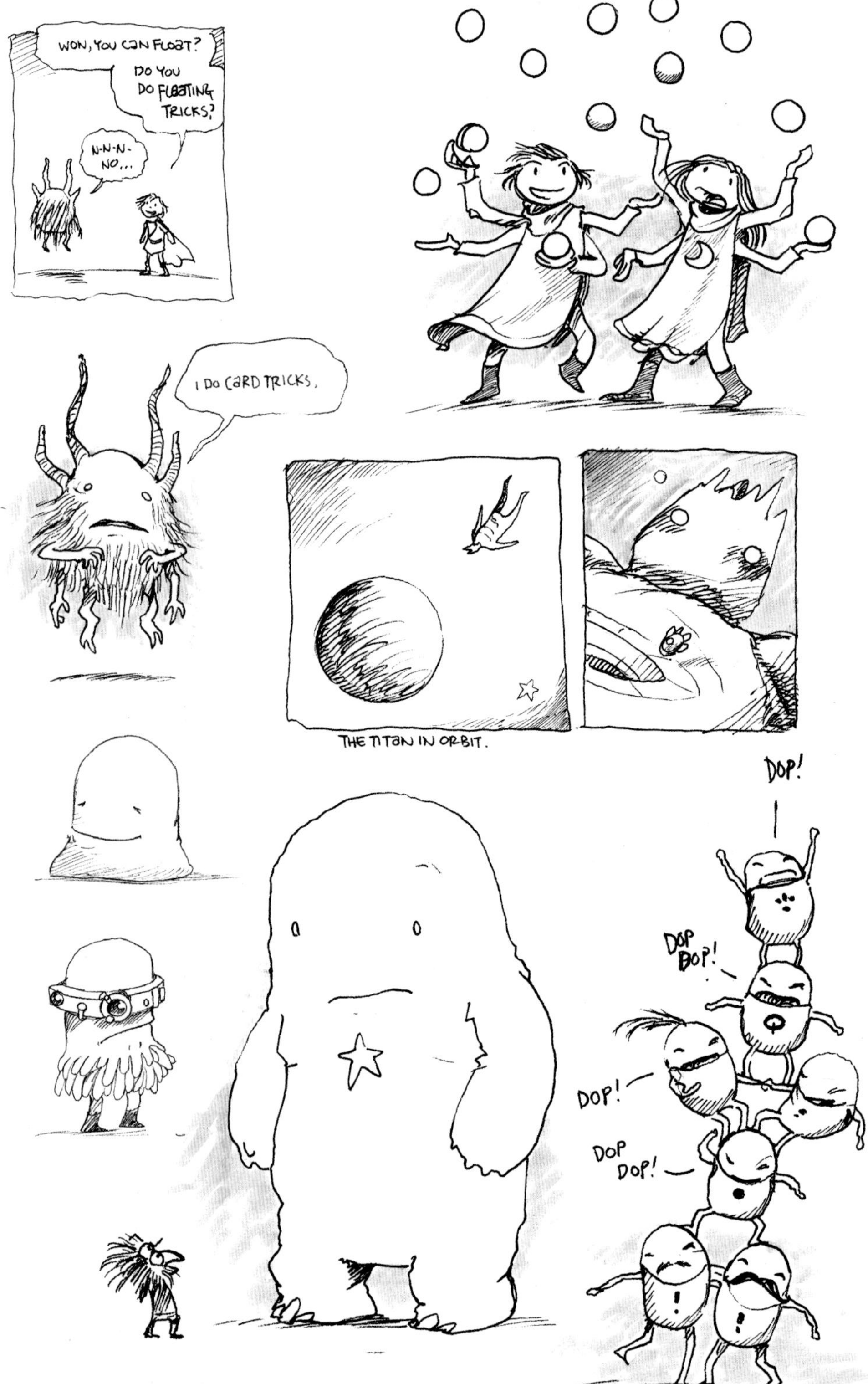

WON, YOU CAN FLOAT?
DO YOU DO FLOATING TRICKS?
N-N-N-NO...
I DO CARD TRICKS.
THE TITAN IN ORBIT.
DOP!
DOP DOP!
DOP!
DOP DOP!

flip
DEN I TODE HIM, I SAY NO ONE KIN FOLLER YER DREAMS BUT YOO!

ACKNOWLEDGMENTS

First and foremost, special thanks go to my lovely wife, Anna, whose patience knows no bounds. Whenever I walk the road of sadness and self-doubt she jumps out from behind a tree of good cheer and throws rocks of encouragement at me. You're the best ever, Anna.

Thanks to my old friends Andy, Ryan, and Bill for reading early drafts. You guys are okay too, I guess.

Thanks to my ever-faithful editor, Kat Kopit, who knows so well how comics work, and thanks to her father, playwright Arthur Kopit, for one special conversation about stories. Thanks to my agent, Judy Hansen, for looking after me. And thanks to Mark Siegel for being not just a publisher, but a fellow artist and a friend.

Finally to my coloring crew! This book would not have made its final deadline if not for Kean Soo, Tory Woolcott, Anthony VanArsdale, Stephanie Yue, and Rosie ("the cat") Schmiedicke. You guys bailed me out.

Oh, and of course to my ever-inspiring daughters, Angelica, Zita, Julia, and Ronia. You four make life fun.

ABOUT THE AUTHOR

Ben Hatke has published comics stories for anthologies, including the Flight series and Explorer. He also keeps a comics journal online, which he gathers into yearly collections. This is his second graphic novel.

Ben lives in Virginia's Shenandoah Valley with his wife, four daughters, a flock of chickens, and a cat. He enjoys juggling, fire-breathing, doing backflips, and rolling 20-sided dice with his friends. Ben's art and journal comics can be seen online at www.benhatke.com.